MARY CRAWFORD

Port in the Storm

A HIDDEN HEARTS NOVELLA 1

COPYRIGHT

Published on November 11, 2016, by Diversity Ink Press and Mary Crawford. Author may be reached at MaryCrawfordAuthor.com.

ISBN: 978-1-945637-38-4

Cover by Covers Unbound

HIDDEN BEAUTY SERIES

Until the Stars Fall from the Sky

So the Heart Can Dance

Joy and Tiers

Love Naturally

Love Seasoned

Love Claimed

If You Knew Me (and other silent musings)
(novella)

Jude's Song

The Price of Freedom (novella)

Paths Not Taken

Dreams Change (novella)

Heart Wish (100% charity release)

Tempting Fate

The Letter

The Power of Will

Hidden Hearts Series

Identity of the Heart

Sheltered Hearts

Hearts of Jade

Port in the Storm (novella)

Love is More Than Skin Deep

Tough

Rectify

Pieces (a crossover novel)

Hearts Set Free

Freedom (a crossover novel)

The Long Road to Love (novella)

Love and Injustice (Protection Unit)

Out of Thin Air (Protection Unit)

Soul Scars (Protection Unit)

OTHER WORKS:

The Power of Dictation

Vision of the Heart

#AmWriting: A Collection of Letters to Benefit The
Wayne Foundation

Dedication

To those who find courage
when you think you have none,
strength when you are at your weakest,
and a voice when you have been silenced —
may we all become your greatest defenders.

CHAPTER ONE

SAM

As I flip through my mail and encounter a greeting card from my friend Jessica; I'm amazed by how much our lives have changed in just a little more than a year. Even when we were working together back in Florida, she was always one to find me silly, whimsical stuff, usually related to my love of sci-fi television shows. However, this time, she is giving me a sneak peek of her choices for her wedding dress. We always joked that if we didn't find someone to marry by the time we were forty, we'd marry each other, but it looks like she's beaten our arbitrary deadline by a long shot. From everything she's told me, Mitch seems like everything she'd always hoped she'd find. I'm thrilled for her. Really. Still, all of her joy doesn't abate my fear that I won't ever follow in her footsteps. I gather up all of my mail and tuck it back into my pack and resume walking toward the MAX train.

A couple lost in a passionate embrace while they're walking down the sidewalk nearly run right into me. I just shake my head at their completely preoccupied state. I wonder if I'll ever be in their shoes. Somehow, I doubt it. Women just don't seem terribly interested in me. Oh, I'm great to hang out with. I'm a wonderful buddy, sounding board, and confidant. Sometimes, if I'm really lucky, they'll cast me as the temporary boyfriend to scare away the guy they're not really interested in. When it comes to being the real thing, not so much.

Of course, things would probably be easier if I could actually express my thoughts in a way other people could understand without having to repeat myself three or four times. I'm a smart guy. Actually, I'm scary smart. The kind of smart they have special organizations for, you know the kind of smart the teachers whisper about in the halls. The only problem is, people don't really know that about me because they don't take enough time to listen to what I have to say. Don't get me wrong, not everybody is like this. There are a few special people in the world like Jessica who look beyond my weird speech, my strange gait and my balance problems which make me look like I'm drunk — but those people are rare. Far more common are the people who think my cerebral palsy is somehow contagious and might affect their kids if they touch me in the grocery store or the teachers who once believed because it took me longer to get to class, I somehow must be stupid and needed remedial special ed. Most days, I try not to let all these assumptions bother me. Still, on a beautiful late spring day like today, when the world seems all coupled up, I can't seem to help but let my mind wander there.

I guess in many ways, I've been pretty lucky. I actually have an employer who has a lot of faith in my abilities. In fact, I just got a huge promotion. I work for Heartbeats in Rock Jewelers; I started as an intern there when I became a gemologist fresh out of college. Jorge was so impressed with my encyclopedic knowledge of gems, he kept me on. Recently, when one of the other stores in the chain showed signs of internal theft, he made me the manager of the store because he knew I could run the business and determine the quality of the merchandise almost by sight. It's been an epic challenge because, understandably, the current staff at the store were not thrilled when someone from the East Coast came in to tell them how to do their jobs. I wasn't offended by their attitudes because I am used to being the newcomer in lots of different situations. My dad was in the Navy, and I've been the newbie more times than I can count. I know how to 'adapt and overcome' as my Dad would say. It didn't take me very long to figure out who the thieving sleaze ball was. She wasn't very careful — more greedy than smart. I'm not sure why she would do that to Jorge because he's quite generous and in the long run, she would have been ahead just to walk the straight-and- narrow.

I have to stop to adjust my backpack, these new forearm crutches are killing me. They have a different type of grip and it's shredding the skin on my palms. Just as I'm trying to pull the sleeves of my sweatshirt down over my hands to afford me a little protection, someone pushes me down from behind. As my head strikes a parking enforcement pole on the way down to the ground, I vaguely wonder if it's the same oblivious couple I saw a few moments ago. I reach up to adjust my glasses on my face and the earpiece comes apart in my hand. I have the world's worst luck. I just got these glasses. I move my hands to my aching head and notice a huge goose egg right smack in the middle of my forehead. "That'll be attractive," I mutter with a sigh.

"Oh, I guess I don't quite have my land legs yet. I'm so sorry," a voice apologizes with a slight Texas twang. "Oh Lord, look what I did to you! They'll probably cancel my shore leave just so I can do paperwork."

Flopping my scraped arms down on my knees, I notice a torn spot on my new jeans. *Not another pair. I should make my life easier and just buy stock in Levi Strauss.* I squint up at her, as I remark, "No need for that. It's not like I don't fall a dozen times a day with no assistance or outside intervention. If you get your friends to give me some leverage to get off the ground, I think I'll survive."

"Are you sure?" she asks, disbelief clear in her voice.

"Positive. Seriously, some days I spend more time on the ground than on my feet. It was probably a coincidence you found me standing when you ran into me. I wouldn't want to interrupt your liberty. My dad was in the Navy and he always told me how much shore leave meant to him. Go enjoy your time with your friends."

"I really think you should let me file a report in case you're hurt, it would be disastrous if you got worse and I did nothing."

"Really, I would feel much worse if you didn't get to enjoy your time here in Portland. I insist. Welcome to Oregon, Sailor. Thank you for your service."

CHAPTER TWO

TAYLOR

"You know there are only so many ways you can artfully arrange things in a duffel bag, right? Besides, we have to wear our whites when we're out in public anyway. It's not like we can shed the Navy altogether and put on a LBD and heels and party hardy," my best friend and bunkmate, Emily remarks as she sees me trying to carefully cram everything I own into my allowable bag.

"Fine, so you have a point, Dodson," I retort, wrinkling my nose. "Did you ever think about the fact that I may actually be excited to be back in Portland? I really loved the city — it is so cool. Did you know they actually have a slogan, 'Keep Portland Weird'. Is that not my kind of city?"

"Actually, it does sound a lot like you," Emily replies with a mischievous twinkle in her eye. "Are you planning to knock down any innocent strangers on this trip?"

"Shut up! It's not like I meant to do it. I was lucky he was so polite about it. Most guys would not be so nice. I was lucky he didn't turn around and deck me."

"Tay, most people in their right minds would not deck you for bumping into them while you were taking a picture. I don't know what kind of men you usually hang out with, but most of them wouldn't deck you for a single mistake." Emily shakes her head.

"You couldn't prove it by me. You obviously haven't met my ex fiancé. Reid Weber considered any contact he didn't initiate to be an offensive touching. Unless he wanted a roll in the sack, I wasn't allowed to touch him for any reason; even if it was an accident. If I did, there were consequences to pay — usually followed by bruising the next day."

"You were going to marry this charmer, why?" Emily probes.

"That would be the billion dollar question, now wouldn't it?" I answer dryly.

"Come on, Taylor, you must have some idea —" Emily continues to push.

I throw my hands up in the air and sigh. "I don't know. I guess I thought he was the opposite of my dad. I watched my dad tear down my mom for years. I thought I'd found the opposite of Dad. When Reid came along, he was thoughtful, kind and attentive. He seemed to like my quirkiness and accept it, which is something my dad never did."

"What happened? How did he turn into a monster?" Emily asks with a look of concentration on her face.

"I ask myself that almost every night. I don't know

if I simply didn't see the signs or if the signs weren't there. Once he had the ring on my finger, it was almost like he underwent a personality change. The guy who was patient and understanding with me and thought everything I did was cute, was completely non-existent. He was irritable and short and a few bricks shy of flat-out lunatic. If I didn't bring him his coffee the exact temperature he preferred it, he would grab the flesh at my waist and twist it so tight I would have bruises for days. He was always very careful to do it where no one could see it unless I took my clothes off. Then, he would tell me, 'I am a very powerful person at work, do you think they're going to believe someone like you? A college student barely out of high school? Someone who's had a traumatic past? Someone whose father killed himself from the guilt?'"

Emily's mouth is hanging wide open and her eyes are as big as saucers. "How did you end up in the Navy, surrounded mostly by men? Weren't you terrified? I mean, for the most part we are trapped on a ship here with them. We have some personal safety training, but we're still at risk."

"My fiancé tortured me because he had the power and it made him feel good that he could abuse me and get away with it. He loved playing God. Reid was the dispatch supervisor, and he was friends with police officers and fire personnel from three counties. They were at his beck and call. I decided I would be safer in the middle of the ocean with a boat full of strange men than I was in my own home. Besides, I figured that the military would teach me how to use weapons and to fight for myself. I never learned that growing up. It was about time for me to learn. I wanted to be able to finish my engineering degree. If I ran from Reid and his richer-than-the-Kardashians family forever, I wouldn't be able to do that. I worked too hard to earn my grades to throw all my dreams away just because some guy with an ego the size of a hot air balloon decided to crush me."

"What a jerk," Emily mutters under her breath.

"In a weird way, the Navy was my ticket to safety. I've never really regretted my decision. Sure, training was tough and my DI tried to wash me out during boot camp because he thought I was too much of a pansy to make it. He never realized the boot camp was easier than what I faced every day at home. So, guess what? I'm still here and he's not because he was caught fraternizing with several other soldiers, despite having a wife and four kids. Maybe he should've focused more on his job and less on his libido."

"Speaking of libido, it's been years since you've been with your 'own personal hell on Earth'. Since you're here in Portland, which is one of your favorite places on the planet, are you going to let your hair down and live it up a little? After all, the last time you were here, you were tackling random guys to get their attention — surely there has to be an easier way to handle it. I think drinking a few margaritas and dancing with a few hot guys would be the way to go. From what I've seen online, they've got the rugged lumberjack look down to a science in Portland; they've got the hot-nerdy-scientist look nailed too. You could probably have your choice," she points out helpfully.

"Emily, I'm not going to go to port and shop for some random guy." I giggle at the thought. "First of all, my luck is far too bad to cast my fate to the wind like that. Secondly, I'm too much of a lady to go trolling through Craigslist ads like a lonely-hearts mail order bride. Can you imagine the type of guy who goes trolling for a sailor? They're looking for somebody, but I'll bet you it's not me. I'm probably a little too straightforward, in-your-face, and take no prisoners. I look cute and all that, but I'm far too scarred by life to fit to be who they're looking for. I don't think we'll have much chance to socialize with the guys in town, anyway. Aren't we scheduled to stay with a group of nuns at a Catholic girls' school?"

"Yeah, that's what I heard too. However, I also heard they had to close it for winter break to repair the pipes. It's probably no big deal. The program always finds new families to host us — the waiting list is a mile long. Although, did I tell you about the ship I was on a couple years ago? This one sailor found his birth family on one of the holiday visits. It was purely accidental, but very cool, nonetheless."

"I didn't hear anything about broken water pipes. Maybe that was just a rumor. Who knows?"

At the moment, the CO arrives on deck. He abruptly points at me. "John, you're up. Ride's here."

Dropping my salute, I ask him, "Dodson too?"

"Nope. Just you. It's your family."

My stomach drops down to my feet — it's all I can do not to pass out. I try to school my expression so I don't betray all the emotions rolling through my mind.

I've been in the Navy since I turned nineteen. I should be beyond this, but I can't help my visceral reaction. I try to take a deep breath and let it out through my nose before I evenly say, "Sir, I have no family."

"Duly noted. I read your file. The host family went through a heightened level of security as a result. Everything checks out."

"I appreciate that, Sir, thank you."

"Enjoy your holiday, John. It's beautiful in Portland this time of year."

Chapter Three

Sam

I've been antsy all day. I was really surprised when they selected my name to host a sailor. I figured they would choose a more traditional family, but perhaps they chose me because of my dad. I remember my dad telling me stories about his time on leave when he got to spend it with different families. Back in those days, they were able to spend several liberty days with different families. The security precautions were a little more lax prior to the terrorist bombing on September 11th. It was on one of those liberties during Fleet Week that my dad met my mom. He was assigned to a family and became good friends with a guy. They became pen pals. The guy kept hassling my dad to meet his sister. As a soldier, my dad was really used to well-meaning suggestions and resisted his friend's efforts. During the second Fleet Week he spent with the host family, she came home from college and my dad pretty much fell in love on the spot. The rest, as they say, is history.

My dad always talked about wanting to host families after he retires from the military, but he and my mom can't agree on how to handle life when he retires, so I'm not sure they'll ever get around to it. I am looking forward to meeting the guy they assigned to me and honoring my family's legacy of respecting the soldiers who serve. My dad doesn't share much about the time he spent in the Navy. It'll be really interesting to hear what life was like for him as a sailor. I think my dad is really disappointed that because of my birth defect, I can't carry on the family tradition of being in the military. I think we missed out on a really important bonding experience.

Unfortunately, I can't get to the area where they are having the rest of the families wait because my scooter won't go there and it's too far for me to walk with my crutches. The organizers of the program have asked me to wait in another area. I'm too nervous to mess around with my cell phone to make it look like I'm doing something productive. When I'm nervous or anxious, my muscles tend to get more spastic, which makes it harder for me to do things which require fine motor control. Instead, I sit and stare out at the harbor and watch the birds fly on and off the docks. It's cold outside, but not bad for December in Oregon — it could be worse.

The big, heavy, metal door opens behind me and I turn around as an officer announces, "Samuel Taylor, thank you so much for opening your home to Petty Officer John."

I have to consciously remember to lift my jaw off the ground when I see who it is. By the look on her face, she seems just as surprised as I am. She quickly collects herself and responds, "We are already pretty well acquainted, Senior Chief."

The officer looks at his watch. "Very well then, I'm late to a briefing. Be back at 1800 hours on the third of January. Conduct becoming, John. Remember that."

She salutes him smartly. "Yes, Senior Chief. Message received. Have a good holiday, sir."

As the door shuts behind her commanding officer with a resounding clank, Officer John looks as nervous as I feel — that is a feat all in itself. I'm pretty sure she can see me trembling. I'm jerking like some deranged marionette. Sometimes I really hate the fact that my cerebral palsy amplifies every emotion and nervous twitch I feel. When I played out all the scenarios I thought might occur today, this was not one of them. I figured they would assign me a geeky single guy who was into computers and studies the ocean bottom or maps or something similar.

The silence is growing awkward, so I start with the obvious, "I have to ask — John?"

Her low husky laugh is like a breeze through a wheat field on a late summer day. "I guess you could say my dad really wanted a boy. The whole thing is only slightly less egregious — Taylor Samantha John."

Everything becomes clear as I remember the paperwork I saw on the organizer's desk. "Oh, that's why they had you down as John Taylor. They probably thought we were related. Believe it or not, my name is Sam John Taylor — actually my full name is Samuel Jonathan Taylor. When I started talking, it took forever to get all the syllables out, so they shortened it to Sam John. My dad's name is Sam too, so they frequently include my middle name just to keep it all straight," I have to catch my breath after saying all that. It takes a massive amount of concentration for me to talk this much. I wait to see what her reaction is. She didn't seem to notice much the first time we met, but the circumstances were incredibly strange that day so I'm not sure what she thought of me that day. It was loud and chaotic out there. Perhaps she didn't hear me or she wasn't actually paying attention.

As I watch her try to untangle my words, she doesn't appear to be put off or unsettled. She just grins. "You probably have the same issue with your first and last name as I do. Did you hate it in school when they couldn't figure out which was your first name and your last?"

"Did you really catch all that or are you simply being polite? I usually have to repeat things three or four times when I'm talking to new people," I explain, unable to curb my curiosity over her unusual reaction.

She shoots me a look of total confusion. "I'm sorry … did you just tell me to be rude to you? I can handle it that way if that's what you really me want me to do. I'd rather not, because I understand you perfectly fine. Compared to my grandma, your speech is crystal-clear. She had a stroke when I was about two, so I pretty much don't remember her talkin' any other way. She liked to joke that we learned to talk together. She would tell my teachers at school it's why I have a strange accent."

"You're right, I jumped the gun. I guess I can be a little defensive about all this. You're not exactly what I expected."

"To be honest, you're not exactly what I expected

either. I was told I was going to stay with a bunch of nuns at a Catholic girls' school," she admits.

"I hope you're not disappointed. Although, I probably will have to change my plans for the week. I figured I would be getting a guy who was an oceanographer or computer geek like me. I suspect you probably won't want to veg out watching old episodes of *Star Trek* and check out ComicCon with me and you're probably not into playing copious amounts of video games."

She sighs as she takes her cap off and recoils the hair at the base of her neck. "For the life of me, I will never figure out why guys always think the only thing women watch are goofy reality shows and soap operas. Where is it written that just because I have ovaries, I can't like a good TV show? For the record, I tend to lean more toward *Firefly*, but I've been known to go old school and watch a little *Star Trek*. I wouldn't call myself a Trekkie, but I wouldn't embarrass you at ComicCon."

"My apologies. It's just that in my experience, women like you only exist in my fantasies. Speaking of that, I know this is totally weird and I swear it's not a come on — but I think I know you. Your voice sounds totally familiar to me."

"It should. I knocked you down on one of the most embarrassing days of my life and I didn't have an opportunity to properly apologize or make it right. I still feel bad about that."

"No, I told you not to worry about that. I didn't even have any lasting bruises — just the stupid scrapes on my hands. I'm talking about before then. I swear you look familiar to me."

"I'm not sure that's possible. You've seen me on both of my trips to Portland. I haven't been here any other time."

"I probably don't even know you from here. I haven't been in Portland long. I'm a newcomer here too. Originally I'm from Tampa."

I've heard the phrase "white as a ghost" before, but until this second, I'd never seen it in real life. I thought for a minute Taylor would pass out on the floor right in front of me. I shift in my scooter seat, pull a bottle of water from my messenger bag and hand it to her.

"What's wrong? Most folks like Florida — you know Mickey and all his pals live there," I tease, hoping to restore the lighthearted mood.

She sets the water down, untouched, on a desk next to her as she looks at me with her eyes still wide with terror as she asks in a raw, broken voice, "I just need to know how much Reid paid you to do this. For some weird, perverse reason, I'd like to know what my sanity is worth on the open market."

Chapter Four

Taylor

WHAT IS IT ABOUT boys that makes me totally stupid? For a few minutes, I let myself believe Sam was different. Actually, I had allowed my fantasy about him to grow since Fleet Week when I unceremoniously ran him over while I was taking pictures. His response to me was so unusual and polite I thought, maybe, just maybe, I had found a diamond in the rough — the one guy who was completely different from anyone else I have ever encountered. I guess I just have the world's worst luck with men. There must be something written on my forehead which says, "Pick this one, she's a pathetic loser." I have to hand it to Reid; he's more devious than ever.

My monster of an ex-fiancé would have had to raise his game to unprecedented levels to manipulate the commanding officers and the volunteer program, not to mention the group that I was sightseeing with the first day when I inadvertently ran into Sam. The number of things which would've had to go absolutely right to make this happen are truly mind-boggling. I still don't know how he did it. It's enough to make me want to throw up. I have sweat pouring off my body from the adrenaline dump. I panic as I realize I have nowhere to stay. My chief is probably in the middle of a high-level briefing right now. My personal crisis is not critical enough to interrupt him. It wouldn't be a stretch to think my ex-fiancé is waiting back wherever Sam lives. I mentally review all the self-defense moves the Navy has taught me and try to remind myself I'm not the same person I was at nineteen.

I will myself to hold it together, as I realize Sam is quietly observing me fall apart right in front of him. I refuse to give him the satisfaction.

"Taylor, I'm not trying to be dense here, but I feel like we must be traveling in some weird parallel universe because I have no idea what you're talking about. I don't know what I did wrong. All I did was mention that you look familiar and that I'm from Tampa. As far as I know, I don't know anybody named Reid."

"You claim to know me, but I don't know you. How did we both wind up in Portland? Why are you the only guy who happens to end up with a female sailor, who just happens to be me — when I've been hiding from my ex-fiancé for years? Don't say coincidence. I'm not buying it."

"I don't blame you for being suspicious. If I were in your shoes, I'd feel the same. Even so, I'm about the most boring person you could ever meet. I moved to Portland because I got a promotion at Heartbeat of the Rock Jewelry, where I've worked since I was about twenty years old and new to the art of being a gemologist. I basically grew up in the Tampa store.

Moving to Portland is pretty much the most adventurous thing I've done."

"The jewelry store," she mutters to herself half under her breath. "I should've known. I don't know why I didn't recognize you sooner. You still look more or less the same. You were a perfect stranger back then, but you were the only person to caution me against marrying Reid. After the break-up, I asked my mom what she thought about it. I was shocked when she admitted she knew he was a jerk and that it would never last — but she was hoping I would get a big wad of money if we ever got divorced."

"Wow! I don't even know your mom, but I think I might hate her just a little. I think I remember you now, but you look a little different. Didn't you have blonde hair back then? I remember thinking your hair didn't match your eyes."

"Reid didn't like me with dark hair," I mumble.

"He disagreed with your DNA? Are you kidding me? That's pretty narcissistic. Anyway, I recall your hair wasn't the only thing which seemed out of place. Your fiancé seemed to take great pleasure in tearing you to pieces over every opinion you had — big or small. I didn't know you at all, but by the time your ring consultation was over, it was all I could do to not-so-politely escort him out of my store. I wanted to grab you by the shoulders and ask you what in the world you were doing.

You should have never been treated that way. Real men

don't treat women like that — but it wasn't my place to say anything. I wanted to take you away from him and tell you that you deserved more."

"If you cared so much about what happened to me, why did you sell me a bogus ring?"

SAM

"WHAT ARE YOU TALKING about? There was nothing bogus about your ring. In fact, when your fiancé chose that particular ring, I thought it was ridiculous. He chose one of the most ostentatious rings in the whole store. Yeah, it was valuable, but he was missing the whole point. It's not uncommon, but I'm not sure if I've ever seen someone devalue their fiancée quite as much as yours did. I was actually embarrassed for you."

"I don't know what to tell you. When I tried to trade my ring in to get cash to escape from Reid, I took it to three different pawnshops and they all told me it was costume jewelry and not worth anything. I was livid because I ended up paying the credit card bill for that worthless ring for years. I just got it paid off a few months ago."

"It's easy enough to trace. The diamond has a laser inscribed serial number in the stone itself. Every time the stone is sold, the serial number is recorded on the bill of sale. In theory, it's supposed to work like the VIN number on a car. I personally inspected and graded the diamond in that ring. I placed it in the box when I sold it to your fiancé. It was in the sack when you guys left the store. What happened to The specific diamond after that is anybody's guess. We should be able to reliably rebuild the history of your stone using the identification number lasered into the stone."

"Wow, I thought diamonds were interchangeable, especially after they had been taken out of their set. Do you really think we have an opportunity to catch that rotten jerk in yet another lie? At this point, I'm going to choose to believe you over him. He has done nothing but lie throughout our whole relationship. This is just one more shining example of his most prominent personality trait," she declares in a disgusted tone. "Every time I think Reid Weber can't stoop any lower, he does … in spectacular fashion."

"With any luck, he may have conned his way into a corner he can't get out of this time. I'll put my loss prevention folks on it on Monday. Technically, I'm off this week for vacation, but we'll go into the store and file your paperwork. I should be able to retrieve the records from Florida using the corporate database. I know you said you ended up with the payments, but do you remember who filled out the financial paperwork with financing?"

"Heck yes, I remember. I was beyond angry. Can you believe I had to pay for my own wedding set after he had purported to be this grand romantic? He gave me this long involved story about why he didn't have his wallet. Apparently, his car was in the shop and the car lot sent it out for detailing — somehow he lost his wallet and could not retrieve his credit card, but didn't discover it until that very moment," Taylor describes the memory with disdain. "He promised to come back to the store and fix the account the next day, which he obviously never did."

"What a prince. Just so you know, not all men are creeps. I don't know if I can do anything, but I'll certainly try. No one deserves to be treated like that. I hope we can nail this guy. In the meantime, welcome back on land — I can't wait to get you back to Portland and show you around the City of Roses — so, what can I do to start things off on a more pleasant note?" I ask, brushing my hands together as if dismissing the whole nasty topic of her ex-fiancé.

"I know this is an odd thing for me to ask, but do you mind if we just randomly take off somewhere? I've heard Oregon is beautiful. I have been cooped up for so long I just want to be on the road and free, I don't really care where at this point — as long as eventually you can point me toward good food, I'll be happy."

"Are you sure you trust me to drive?" I ask as I turn on the scooter.

"As long as you don't want me to ride piggyback on the freeway on that thing, I suppose I do," she answers with a healthy degree of skepticism.

"Are you kidding? People around here drive like maniacs! You'd need a seatbelt and I don't have a spare." I look up at her and grin "I drive a nice safe minivan like a soccer mom."

CHAPTER SIX

TAYLOR

Honestly, I didn't know quite what to expect, especially after learning Sam was from Tampa. I really almost lost it. After I figured out who he really was, I realize the chances he's an ally rather than the enemy are pretty good. I decided to trust my gut for whatever that's worth. It's still a frightening proposition since my gut has let me down before. Under the circumstances, I really don't have much choice.

The Pacific Northwest sure lives up to its billing. The first thing that hits me is the fact that there are trees everywhere. It looks like a Christmas tree farm exploded. As soon as we leave the congestion of the naval base in Washington and head toward Portland, everywhere I look there are large trees and they look nothing like the trees in Florida. Sam explains if we want to go to Eastern Oregon, there is a mountain range where people go skiing. I pull out my cellphone and take pictures of the snow-capped mountains. Even in the middle of the day, it looks like something you'd see on a postcard.

When Sam told me where he lived, I was dreading the almost three-hour drive with someone I didn't know, but Sam is refreshingly honest in a way which tells me he spends a lot of time watching people. My grandmother would have loved him and I'm sure they would've spent a lot of time comparing notes. He pulls no punches when it comes to calling people out on fake behavior and his commentary is touchingly funny. I can't remember laughing this hard in a long time. He has an odd way of encouraging me to open up and talk about myself. I haven't felt this comfortable since before I met Reid.

I'm not sure what I find most appealing about him. It could be that he is really smart and funny but doesn't find it necessary to go out of his way to convince me; or maybe it's because he isn't trying to show me how brave and macho he is every other second. Perhaps it's because he seems to value my opinion about things. It doesn't seem to matter whether it's something trivial like what makes a standup comedian funny or something serious like global politics, Sam seems genuinely interested in what I think about things. Even if we disagree, he doesn't challenge my opinion simply for the purpose of proving me wrong or making me feel inferior.

Theoretically, I know this is how friendships are supposed to work in the real world. But since Reid did a number on me, I haven't felt comfortable enough to let my guard down. It's nice to feel like the person I was before someone set out to destroy my soul.

Instead of sightseeing today, I elected to stay in. Even though Sam has said nothing, I can tell his muscles must be sore. Today, while we were at Powell's bookstore, the mechanism which lifts the scooter in and out of Sam's van broke down. Fortunately, I was able to run to an auto supply store and grab the parts I needed to fix it. Sometimes, having a degree in engineering is helpful. A lot of guys are threatened by what I do, but Sam was gracious. He thanked me for my help and told me I saved him a lot of money. Unfortunately, while his scooter was in the van, he was using his crutches and the added pressure broke open an existing blister on his hand. He didn't say a word, but I could tell it was causing him a great deal of pain. In an effort to help reduce his pain, I volunteered to make dinner tonight.

"How do you feel about mushrooms?" I yell into the living room.

"Knock yourself out," Sam replies, "but I hate those bamboo things."

"You're in luck, I hate them too. Pea pods?" I ask.

"I have no opinion about pea pods," he responds.

"Okay, I'm adding them for your health — besides, every good stir-fry has pea pods."

After I finish the stir-fry, I dish it up on a couple plates and carry them into the living room. Poor Sam, he looks half-sacked out on the sofa, but when he sees me, he sits up and says, "You didn't have to wait on me. Cooking dinner was more than enough."

"Don't worry about it. Whenever I'm not deployed, I always eat in front of the TV. Unless I'm having company, my table usually is the place where my junk mail lives."

"I know this will sound like a stupid question, but are you gone a lot?"

"It depends on the conflicts around the world. Sometimes I'm gone more than others. Why?"

"You'll probably think this is silly, but you know my dad was in the Navy and he seemed to be deployed all the time. My mom admitted once that my dad never dealt well with my disability. When I was growing up, I often wondered if my dad was gone so much as a coping mechanism of sorts. I'm not saying my logic is very sound, I just can't help but wonder. I had other friends in high school whose parents were in the military. Their parents weren't gone nearly as much as my dad. It was hard not to take it personally on some level."

"I understand. I take a lot of the decisions my parents made far too personally as well. Since I don't know your father and I don't know the circumstances under which he served, I can't pinpoint an answer for you. Didn't your dad serve during the major Gulf conflicts? I think the usual rules go out the window under those conditions. I'm sorry though, that must've sucked for you."

"It did, but I have to remember that it was a lot worse for other people. What do you guys do on the ship? Don't you get bored in your downtime?"

"Sure. There are a bunch of gym rats and a group of poets and writers who got together and published a book. There's this one guy who really should work at Pixar Studios because he is a great cartoonist. He's drawn so many caricatures of all of us he could probably do his own little mini movie. You just find something to do.   I'm in a Trivial Pursuit league. I taught myself how to crochet with videos I found on the Internet. It isn't gorgeous, but it keeps me busy. I read a lot and I happen to think the e-reader is the best invention ever, outside of the personal computer," I answer, pointing to the case sticking out of my purse.

"We should swap reading lists sometime, I read a lot too. Although, I would've never guessed that you'd be into Trivial Pursuit."

I grin. "I guess you could say I play a little. You're looking at the second-place champion. I would have been in first place, but I had to back off because the current reigning champ is one of my superior officers and he wouldn't take kindly to an enlisted chick dressing him down, even if it's for fun and games, so I settled for second — although I would've had no trouble beating him."

Sam straightens his spine and rubs his neck, "I'll tell you what. How about we play ourselves a little game? We'll even let the game console keep score. You play as hard as you possibly can, no holding back to save my ego, promise? Although, I have to warn you, no one has beaten me at this game since I was nine."

I raise an eyebrow at him. "No one? Why haven't you tried out for one of those game shows and made a ton of money?"

"It's weird. Casting directors get all bent out of shape when you can't talk well. Having to repeat myself several times to be understood doesn't play so well on TV."

"Oh, I see. Well, for this game, there is no clock. It's just our skill against the game. If I win, I'll act as your own personal masseuse and work on your sore neck and shoulders," I announce.

Sam is silent for a full minute before he turns to me and says, "Ditto."

I wink at him before I whisper softly, "Okay, Samuel Jonathan Taylor let the games begin."

CHAPTER SEVEN

SAM

SHE BEAT ME. SHE flat out beat me — and it was the sexiest thing I've ever seen in my life. Who knew nave plates and hubcaps were the same thing? Taylor thought that perhaps I took it easy on her so she could win, but I honestly didn't know the answer. Even before she gave me the single best massage I've ever had in my lifetime, I can't remember having so much fun with someone. I told her that after she worked so hard to beat me at the trivia game; she deserved a massage too.

For a woman with extensive self-defense training, Taylor is remarkably ticklish. Every time I'd reach out toward her to give her massage, she would laugh which would cause me to have a spastic reaction. My reaction would cause her to flinch, which would make me flinch too which would make her laugh even harder. Finally, I did what any self-respecting man would do. I took off my glasses and kissed her. It wasn't something I planned in advance; it just seemed to fit the moment. Usually, I get so nervous about this kind of stuff that I can't relax and enjoy myself. But between the two of us, it was a natural extension of where our conversation and activities left off. There didn't seem to be any dramatic buildup or expectation. It was as if one thing flowed into another.

After one intense kissing session, where we both were struggling to catch our breath, she whispered, "I think the glasses are sexy, but I never realized how gorgeous your eyes are."

I'm not quite sure how to answer. It's pretty unusual for women to notice me at all. I don't recall anyone ever mentioning my eyes or any other body parts. I feel my face grow hot with embarrassment. "Thank you, I guess."

Taylor quirked the side of her mouth up as she inquired, "Am I not supposed to think you're handsome?"

"It'll take a little getting used to, but I suppose there are worse things."

Taylor brushes my hair back from my eyes. "Why are you so embarrassed? I think you're handsome."

"If I told you, I'd be even more embarrassed," I admit as I feel my face grow hot under her fingers.

She traces a scar with her thumbnail. "What happened here?"

I flinch at the memory. "When I was in the fourth grade, I lost my balance and bumped into the wall at my grandma's house and a picture fell and the glass cut my face."

Taylor winces in sympathy. "That must've hurt. It makes you look rugged though."

"Thanks … I think. I'm not sure anybody's ever noticed before."

"Really? None of your other girlfriends have said anything about your gorgeous eyes?"

I close my eyes out of sheer embarrassment.

"Honestly, I don't do a lot of dating. I'm kind of a nerdy guy. I'm kind of the guy people go out with to scare off guys they're not interested in. My friend, Jessica from work, used to hang out with me just for fun, but I was never her serious boyfriend or anything. So, all this is really strange territory for me."

"Huh…" Taylor says before she leans down and kisses me. "The girls you hang out with must be both blind and stupid. You are one of the coolest guys I've hung out with in a long time."

I gaze up at her beautiful smile and flashing dimples. "Okay, turnabout is fair play. It's been a long time since you broke up with your creepy fiancé. Who have you been dating?"

Taylor sighs. "Nobody much. Every once in a while somebody sets me up on a blind date. But most of the time I try to avoid dating like it's a plague. You can't blame me, my luck has been abysmal at best."

I snicker. "I can't disagree with you. If I'd gone through what you went through, I'm not sure I would've been able to find the strength to get out of bed." I shift around and sit up so I can face her. It takes me much longer than I'm comfortable with — and there's nothing graceful about it. I feel like a turtle who has been knocked over on his back in hot asphalt. There is definitely nothing sexy about my moves. Fortunately, Taylor doesn't seem to even notice. She simply helps me sit up and waits for me to catch my breath so I can continue the conversation.

Facing her, I ask, "So, what do you call what's going on between us?"

Taylor swallows hard. "Do we have to call it anything?"

My heart pounds and blood rushes in my ears as I contemplate what her words might mean.

"I suppose not," I whisper in a hoarse voice, unable to keep my sadness from leaking through.

Taylor watches my expression with alarm.

"Oh no! I didn't mean that the way I think you took it. I just meant this is like a dream. I never want to wake up. At some point I'll have to go back to my real life — and for the first time ever I'd rather not."

As we wait for the waitress to bring back our check, I ask, "So, what did you think?"

"I never would've thought to eat savory crêpes, but it was amazing," Taylor answers.

"I keep trying to tell you, there's more to Portland than Voodoo Donuts. Le Happy is one of my go to places. I have to ask, if you liked it, why do you look like you're about to pass out?"

"You don't understand. When I had to leave, I had to leave everything behind. Reid knew everybody. What's to say he didn't change the paperwork to say I never bought the ring? What if I can't prove it and I'm out nine thousand dollars for the stupid piece of carbon which represented nothing but empty promises and pain?"

"Taylor, with the way our records work within my company, something like that simply can't happen. Our corporate folks won't want an unhappy customer on their hands. They'll likely work with you to help recover it. If they don't, I know who will."

Clicking my phone case shut, I turn to Taylor, pulling her attention away from the bright Christmas displays in Pioneer Courthouse Square. "I know you were frustrated this morning when our folks at the jewelry store said they wouldn't be able to do much except provide copies of your paperwork. To be honest, so was I — but, fortunately, it wasn't my only plan of attack. Remember I told you about my friend Jessica from Florida? We used to work together — well, that's not exactly right — she worked in the same mall and we used to take our lunches together. Anyway, she has more connections than God. Her fiancé, Mitch, works with some high-powered law enforcement guys. It turns out your ex is not unknown within law enforcement circles He's been running sweetheart swindles for a while."

"You mean I wasn't his first sucker?" Taylor asks sardonically.

Mary Crawford

I pull her down onto my lap and kiss her before I
answer, "No, but you'll be the last."

CHAPTER EIGHT

TAYLOR

I PAUSE AS I place silverware on the table. "How many people did you say are coming? Do they usually just show up out of the blue like this? It just seems weird to me," I comment before I can stop the words from flying out of my mouth.

Sam laughs when he sees the horrified expression on my face. "No, I totally agree. It's bizarre. I still don't know how Jessica gets used to that lifestyle. Her fiancé works for Tristan. I guess Tristan invented several kinds of famous software and he owns one of those Internet security firms which hunts down hackers and stuff like that. He married Rogue and her father-in-law is a legendary law enforcement guy with the feds."

"That's all very fascinating, but it doesn't explain why they're coming the day after Christmas?"

"Oh, that … Well, the official story line is they are coming because Jessica never got to say goodbye when she moved to Kansas and that she and Ivy — Rogue's twin sister — were checking out where I live and decided they wanted to come see the zoo lights at

Christmas time. I think there's probably a lot more to the story, but we won't know until they get here," Sam answers carefully — a little too carefully. I spend my days around military types who need to keep secrets for a living, so I recognize cagey behavior when I see it — it doesn't make me happy. Still, I don't know what he's been told.

"We're having nine people for dinner?" I ask, looking around his modest home trying to mentally map it out.

"Actually, it's ten, Rosa is coming — she's Isaac's wife."

"Great. I haven't cooked in months and this is the first meal you throw at me? Nothing like a logistical challenge," I reply as I pretend to snap him with the dishtowel.

Sam blocks it with his forearm crutch and grins at me as he replies, "I'm not worried. I've had your cooking before, and it was delicious. If the smells coming out of the kitchen are anything to go by, it'll be perfect."

I know it's easy for me to forget how much military life has changed me, but it's been a long time since I've been around civilians. I have to admit, if I ever had a sister, I would want her to be just like Jessica. She makes it impossible to feel excluded or out of place. She even has me half convinced to go see a classical music concert. I'm not exactly sure how she got me to do that.

After Sam brings out the apple pie we made together this afternoon, Isaac addresses me, "You've been far more patient than I would ever be. As you may have guessed, we have more than one purpose here."

I can feel my heart rate speed up and a light sheen of sweat appears on my forehead as I hear those words. I have no idea what type of news he could be bringing. Before today, I've never even met these people.

"Just tell me," I answer robotically. I'm so used to soul shattering news about Reid Weber, I almost don't have a reflex against it anymore.

"From the look on your face, I don't think our news is anything like what you're expecting," Jessica's friend, Tristan comments as he leafs through a thick file. "Your would-be Casanova has a bit of history with the ladies and hasn't bothered to hide his digital footprint very well. How he got hired by the county as a dispatching supervisor is beyond me."

"You actually know where the slime ball is?" Sam asks incredulously.

"Actually, it was not hard to find him. He was still doing the same type of work; he was just over the county line in the next state."

I roll my eyes as I mutter, "Great, he's got even more cops in his back pocket. No one will ever believe me now."

"Officer John, I don't think that'll be a problem. It seems your ex-fiancé had a little hobby of photographing his victims and sharing them on a website with a bunch of people who are just as sick as he is. Unfortunately for him, he forgot to wipe the metadata off of his photos first. My FBI buddies were able to match the photos online to a camera in his possession."

My eyes widen and I gasp a little as I ask, "Have you already confronted him?"

Isaac chuckles a little as he responds, "To be honest, we didn't get very many words in, he was too busy spouting off. In a manner of speaking, we did speak to him. Mitch happened to have his search and rescue dog, Hope, with him when he and Jessica came to Gainesville. He's been cross training her on some narcotics tasks, so we brought her along with us. Let's just say she took an instant dislike to your ex and was looking especially menacing."

Glancing over at Sam, who is using the tip of his crutch to give the German Shepherd a belly rub, I look back at Mitch and comment, "Somehow I have a hard time reconciling the word menacing and this puddle of furry love."

Jessica giggles and responds in a stage whisper, "Sometime when the guys aren't around for their egos to be crushed, remind me to tell you about the day that I met my fiancé."

Much to my shock, Mitch sticks his tongue out at Jessica and then looks at me and continues, "Anyway, as I was saying, your ex-fiancé wet his pants a little and turned over some cocaine. After we explained why we were there, he handed over the diamond."

"That jerk had it all along? Reid told me he gave it back! If I'd known, I wouldn't have made a fool out of myself at all those pawnshops trying to sell my ring.

Now what happens?" I ask, barely able to keep the rage out of my voice.

"With the holidays, he won't be arraigned until Monday, but they'll do it via closed-circuit television. I've made arrangements with the FBI for you to make a visual I.D. just to confirm what we know from the DNA. The truth is, that boy has bigger problems than stealing your ring from you — but your testimony will be important too. More than likely, he'll go back to jail on the probation violation from his attempted murder charge out of Wisconsin."

"His what?" I hiss, as the horror of his words sink in.

"The routine he pulled with you was not new, but the victim before you was not quite as lucky and she's still recovering from a traumatic brain injury courtesy of your ex. He fled from Wisconsin and got a job with the county before they were finished investigating the crime. Unfortunately, she didn't regain consciousness for several weeks after the incident and even after that, she lost her memory for a while. By the time the law enforcement agency could reconstruct the crime, your fiancé had simply moved to another state and was lying low. When he felt it was safe, he found another job using a different name. Since he still used all the same websites and social media settings, all the money he used to pay off people to hide became meaningless."

"What about his rich family? Couldn't they bail him out?"

"As fake as his good, upstanding morals, I'm afraid," Isaac confirms.

I collapse against the back of the chair in a fit of hysterical giggles. "I was a couple of months away from marrying a total psychopath. What does that say about me?"

"Nothing. It says nothing except you were young, naïve, and not expecting someone to totally take advantage of you. You are smart and beautiful and didn't deserve what was done to you," Sam assures me, as he tries to warm my suddenly cold hands between his.

CHAPTER NINE

SAM

As I watch Jessica and Taylor walk away, it's easy to imagine Taylor staying in my life forever. Her eyes are sparkling with mirth as she laughs at something Jessica says while they are feeding a baby goat in the petting zoo. Without question, this has been the best week of my life and I don't want it to end. Just like we've done every day since she's been here, Taylor and I talked for hours until the sun came up after we took a tour of the Christmas lights on Peacock Lane. She probably knows more about me than any person on the planet. This is how I always thought a relationship with someone should be, but I'm still having a hard time believing this is my life.

Our relationship has been an incredible whirlwind. In my wildest dreams, I never expected for history to repeat itself. I never understood how my dad could fall for my mom in just a few days, yet I am in the same situation. Taylor is everything I ever wanted in a partner.

She's smart, funny, and she doesn't seem to even notice my disability much. If she does, she doesn't make a huge deal out of it.

"Hey, weren't you supposed to be taking pictures?" Jessica asks as she gently pokes me in the shoulder interrupting my thoughts.

"I was," I admit. "I got distracted."

"Not that you asked my opinion, but I think Taylor is the perfect distraction for you. You guys are great together. In all the years I've known you, I've never seen you so happy."

"Did you feed her to the lions or something?" I ask, looking around.

Jessica shudders as she answers, "No, she and Mitch wanted to go look at something which requires climbing in high places and you know how I am about heights. Quit trying to change the subject, Sam. It's nothing bad. I was just trying to say I'm thrilled for you guys. You seem like you are in a great place."

"Do you really think we're in such a great place? I mean, she's leaving. We haven't even specifically talked about whether she feels the same way I do."

Jessica ducks her head close to mine and speaks in a soft, but intense voice, "Sam, I've never pulled any punches with you. Over the past few days, your girlfriend and I have been talking like long-lost best friends. What you guys have has taken her completely off guard. She's understandably nervous after what she's been through. Taylor says she's never had anyone like you in her life — as a lover or anything else."

I blush clear to the roots of my hair. "Come on Jess, you're just messing with me. There's no way you guys talked about those kinds of details. I figured she would keep that stuff between us."

"In her defense, I'm pretty good at getting people to tell me stuff that they don't plan to. My grandpa is a pastor, remember? I learned from the best. You don't need to worry, Sam; everything she told me came from a place of love and acceptance. She loves you like Mitch loves me."

"How can it possibly work? She's leaving in just a few days. Who falls in love so quickly?"

"Who says there has to be a time limit? When it's right, it's right. I knew there was something different about Mitch when I saw his picture on an online dating profile."

"I forgot about that. What about the fact that she's leaving? How can our relationship survive that?"

"Everybody's life has a little crazy in it. It has been insane with Mitch setting up Hope's Haven in Kansas while working with Tristan and Isaac in Florida. All I can say is thank goodness Tristan has his own plane. Still, the time Mitch spends away from Kansas is very hard. We just have to love each other fiercely when we're together and hope someday it will settle down."

As I watch Mitch and Taylor walk towards us pointing to something on Mitch's cell phone, I murmur to Jessica, "With all the stuff that's going on, I pray hope and love are enough."

Taylor looks up at me and scrutinizes me carefully before asking, "What are you guys doing?"

Looking at her steadily, I answer, "Planning for the future."

Taylor looks back and forth between Jessica and me with a curious, almost hostile expression, as she retorts, "That's funny, I could've sworn Jessica already has a future planned with Mitch."

"Taylor, I was telling Jessica about what we talked about last night. I was telling her as improbable as it seems, I love you and want to try to figure out how to make it all work between us."

She sinks down on the bench next to my scooter and exclaims, "Samuel Jonathan Taylor! You about gave me a heart attack. I've been so afraid this is too good to be true that I was waiting for the other shoe to drop. Do you mean it? Is this for real?"

"For me, it's as real as it gets. We just have to work out the details."

Taylor grins at me with tears in her eyes as she responds, "You do get the irony in all this? If we do this thing right, eventually my name will be Taylor Taylor when it's all said and done. I'll go from being the butt of bathroom jokes to something like a fancy law firm."

"Works for me," I say, as I pull her into my lap and kiss her, much to the delight of Jessica who is happily taking pictures with her cellphone.

"You know what? It works surprisingly well for me too. I'm so glad I didn't decide to stay on the ship that day. I love you, Sam John."

Chapter Ten

Taylor

I SWEAR I'M GOING to throw up. If Sam's hand wasn't at the small of my back as he carefully drives his scooter beside me, I still might. I really thought I would pass out when we drove up to the big red building where the FBI is housed. It reminded me so much of the jail where I had to regularly visit my dad before he committed suicide after he fractured my mom's eye socket. The sensory memories were so strong I struggled to breathe through them. The birds even sound the same. Sam senses my distress and helps me with a few meditation techniques. He explains he sometimes uses the breathing exercises to get through very intense muscle spasms.

When we enter the conference room, Tristan and Isaac are already there, dressed in suits. It's actually the first time I've seen Isaac look intimidating. Isaac clears a spot for Sam to sit beside me and he sits on the other side with Tristan sitting across from me. I feel like they've given me a barrier of protection from the unknown agents.

It takes several minutes for the courtroom staff in Florida to get the technology working, but once they do, I can't stop my involuntary recoil as Reid Weber's face comes up bigger than life on the large TV. I flinch as the blood drains out of my face.

Sam squeezes my knee as he whispers, "3,050 miles and a lifetime ago."

I take a drink of ice water and compose myself as I announce, "That's Reid Weber, crooked hair plugs and all. You'll find a visible scar in front of his left ear. He says it's from playing baseball as a kid, but in light of what I've been told, it might actually be a plastic surgery scar."

An agent turns to me. "I forgot to tell you. Mr. Weber can hear everything you just said and it'll be part of the court record."

"I assumed what I said would be under oath. I'm not afraid of the truth," I answer with more confidence than I feel.

Those words seem to shatter whatever composure Reid was struggling to maintain as he screeches at me, "You ungrateful little twit! I knew I should've fenced your freakin' ring but I couldn't get any pawnshops to cut off the stupid inventory number."

Just then, the closed-circuit connection is abruptly cut off.

I glance up at the agent. "Is he under oath too?"

Tristan grins at me. "He is."

I roll my eyes and shake my head. "Does he know that?"

Tristan chuckles. "I never said the man was bright."

After several minutes of tense waiting, the senior agent checks his phone and then closes the file in front of him. He abruptly dismisses me, "Petty Officer John, it appears your work here is done today; thank you for your time. The district attorney already has your affidavit."

As everyone is shuffling paperwork and preparing to leave, about a dozen cellphones go off, including mine. Tristan and Isaac manage to answer their phones first. Isaac scowls as he reads his phone. He looks up at me with a somber expression as he asks, "Do you have your go bag in the van?"

Something in his tone makes me stand at attention as I admit, "No sir. I wasn't expecting liberty to be over for several more days."

"If I don't miss my guess, that message on your phone is the same one I got. I think your holiday leave has officially been canceled. You probably should go get your bag and say your goodbyes for now."

CHAPTER ELEVEN

SAM

I WATCH IN DUMBFOUNDED disbelief as controlled chaos erupts around me. Yet, as tense and harried as it seems, I appeared to be the only person who is clueless about what's happening. It reminds me of when I was younger and my dad would be abruptly deployed with no notice. *Crap*! I don't know how I could be so clueless. It's not as if I'm not a military brat. That's exactly what's happening here. I don't know why I didn't figure it out sooner. I guess I was just focused on keeping Taylor safe and away from Reid Weber.

It's too early for the fairytale to be over. I want to scream at the top of my lungs. I just found her! How can this be happening? It's like a bad movie.

I'm so stunned I can't move. Isaac comes in lays a hand on my shoulder. "Son, you need to pull yourself together. We may not be able to tell you what's going on, but your woman over there will still need you in her corner. Your relationship may be new, but that doesn't mean it's not the real thing. I met my Rosa in the middle of a mission and I knew I would love her forever. So, don't let the timing of this throw you off."

There's something about Isaac's bearing which makes it impossible for you unravel in his presence.

I sit up straight and draw in a deep breath. "Yes sir, understood. Message received on all fronts."

"What time do you have to report back at base?" I ask as Taylor dries her hair and puts on her uniform.

She wipes away a tear as she shakily responds, "0600 hours. In the whole time I've been in the Navy, I've never dreaded anything quite as much as much. For the first time ever, there is some place else I'd rather be." Taylor slides into my lap and kisses me deeply. "I don't want to leave these arms. I like the way you make me feel."

"In a perfect world, we wouldn't have to make this choice, but this isn't a perfect world. My arms are always open for you."

The ride back to the Naval base in Washington is weirdly electric. It seems as if we both know we have so much to say and no time to say it. We are both lost in our thoughts, yet eager to say a lifetime of words in case we don't get another chance. I can't seem to formulate my thoughts coherently, I don't know if it's the same for her — but I suspect it is.

"From the moment I joined the Navy, the ship has felt like home. It was the place I wanted to be, my safe-haven from a world of violence and fear I didn't understand — but you helped me face down the monster in my dreams and nightmares and put my past where it belongs. For the first time, I can dream of the future again, a better future than I ever envisioned. As corny as this sounds, you have become my port in the storm, my safe place to be. Will you be here when I get back?" Taylor asks, her voice trembling with emotion.

Taylor flashes her I.D. at the security guard on base and I pull my car into the parking spot. I reach into my coat pocket and pull out a box. "I know that these aren't the circumstances under which I wanted to do this and I know you've had a tough history with rings. Let me tell you why I chose this one. This is a virtually unbreakable titanium ring — like the bond between the two of us. I know we haven't known each other long, but even in Florida I felt a pull towards you, even when another man was prepared to put a ring on your finger. I have never met another person who has as much in common with me, yet can challenge me at the same time."

Taylor laughs softly as she declares, "I promise you as many rematches as you need to beat me at Trivial Pursuit."

I smile as I continue, "When we work with gems, we often work with counterweights. It is like your heart and soul are the perfect counterweight to mine. We met under the most unlikely circumstances. Some people might consider it a mistake. I'm not a big believer in mistakes. There was a purpose behind everything that happened to us. I want to give you this ring to remind you of the promise of my love."

Taylor's hand is shaking as she holds it out for me to slide the ring on. "I love the ring. More importantly, I love you. I will be home eventually and then we can build a future together. You are the best thing that's ever happened to me. I'm not going to let a little time and distance come between us. As they say, keep the home fires burning."

I place the ring on her finger and kiss her knuckles. "I never planned to do anything else. I think I fell in love with you the first time I saw you. For love like that, I'll wait a lifetime."

EPILOGUE

TAYLOR

FOR ONCE IN MY naval career, I have someone at the bottom of the ramp waiting for me at the end of a deployment. I always thought those vintage pictures from *Life Magazine* showing sailors being reunited with their families were so romantic. Now, I am about to reenact one.

When I first met Sam, I have to admit I thought all of this was too good to be true. In my experience, men like him just don't exist in my world. I thought Reid Weber had destroyed my ability to love anyone. Yet, Sam has taken the time to rebuild me and my ability to trust. Over the past few months with the help of the U.S. Postal Service, Facebook and Skype, we've been able to fill in much of our relationship that we skipped over during our whirlwind week long courtship. The more I find out about Sam Taylor, the more there is to like — or more precisely — love.

Still, I can't believe that I fell in love in such an unconventional manner with such an unusual man. But the truth is, I've never been happier in my whole life. My friend Emily jokes about it all the time. She says she's planning to start randomly pushing men down on the sidewalk just to see if she can find a guy as nice as Sam.

I peer over the railing and my heart skips a beat when I see the scene unfold in front of me. I can't believe Sam drove all the way to California to meet the ship. He is decked out in a suit with a huge bouquet of red roses. I run my thumb over the edge of my promise ring. The past several months have reinforced my initial feelings for Sam and made them even deeper. I chose the right guy or the right guy chose me. I'm not actually sure how all that works. Still, for all the pain and rotten, terrible luck both of us have had in our lives, something seems to have worked out for us this time.

As I get closer, I watch as he unfurls a banner above his head, which reads, "Petty Officer John, are you ready to be Taylor Taylor?"

For a moment, all the air leaves my lungs. In another time and another place I have been in this position before — but Samuel is not Reid Weber. He helped me catch the man who made my life miserable. Samuel John Taylor is the man who helped me find my strength again. He will be a true partner. So, in the instant that my brain catches up with my heart, there is only one answer to give and I shout it in a loud, clear voice, "Yes, of course — for as many light years as you can count, Samuel John Taylor."

Sam turns to the crowd who are clapping wildly

and says, "See? Didn't I tell you she was perfect for me?"

I passionately kiss him until I accidentally lean against the horn on his scooter causing it to beep. I bow when the crowd laughs. "As you can see, he's perfect for me too."

I watch nervously as the ramp jerks before the door closes on the rental van. Only after it completely closes do I relax and throw my gear in the back of the van. After I climb in the passenger seat and put my seatbelt on, I lean over and kiss Sam again. "Geez, I can't believe it took so long to get through that crowd. I've been counting down the days, hours and minutes, until we can go home."

To me it looks like Sam is holding his breath. I don't blame him. I've been keeping him in limbo. Heck, I've been keeping myself in limbo. This is the toughest thing I've ever had to decide. When we stop at a stoplight, Sam pivots his head toward me sharply and addresses the hard question. "What did you decide?"

"My Chief is not a happy camper, but this is the last time you'll ever have to come pick me up after a mission."

Sam grins widely. "I know this decision wasn't easy and I probably shouldn't be completely over-the-moon happy, but I've missed you so much I can't even pretend I'm sorry that you've decided to retire."

I choke back a laugh. "Retire! It's a good thing my

grandparents aren't alive because they would be mortified. I'm not even thirty." I gaze out the window. "Sam… Are you sure we're going the right way? That sign says we're going south. Last I checked, Oregon was north of San Diego."

Sam shrugs. "I figured since we are both footloose and fancy free for a while I'd add a few extra stops. Do you mind?"

"No, I guess not. I'm not sure what I plan to do. It's weird. The Navy got nine years of my life and was a safe place for me when the outside world was scary, but now I'm ready to define myself on my terms."

Sam opens his mouth and closes it and then opens it again before he says, "I don't know. I think there's a flaw in your logic. You've been defining yourself on your own terms for a long time. Perhaps you've been using the structure of the Navy's as a tool, but you left a terribly abusive relationship and came out the winner. Not only that, you are a respected, decorated officer in the Navy who is retiring with honor. It doesn't get much better than that."

I still get emotional when I hear Sam recount my journey through his eyes. "Thank you. Sometimes it's hard for me to remember the victories. It's easier to remember the pain. Speaking of victories, how about your promotion? Mr. VP of Asset Acquisitions — the youngest one ever!"

Sam pulls on his collar and shifts uncomfortably. "I know. I was shocked Jorge made that move. I would've never guessed when I first started working at

Heartbeats in Rock Jewelers that someday I would be upper management."

"I'm sorry I was deployed when your parents passed and they weren't able to see your big promotion."

"It's all right. I knew my mom wouldn't last long once my dad had his massive stroke. At least they're not in pain any longer."

We were so busy talking I didn't realize that Sam had taken the exit to Coronado until we pull up to a seemingly random convenience store. "I'm sorry I didn't plan ahead for this part." He reaches behind him and pulls a garment bag off of the hook behind the driver's seat. "Jessica says she's sorry she can't be here — but your grandmother would approve."

"What are you talking about?"

"Remember the banner?" Sam asks, his speech slurred by nerves. "You know, Taylor Taylor?"

"You meant today?" I reply with my jaw slack with shock.

Sam nods. "Didn't you?"

"Well, I did say I wanted to define my life on my terms. Getting married would certainly qualify."

Staring back at my reflection in the small vanity mirror on the visor in the van. I wonder how in the world Jessica Campbell pulled this off. I am the spitting image of my grandmother's wedding pictures right down to the tea-length wedding dress and bright red lipstick. It's not a look I would typically wear, but I am so honored to carry on my grandmother's tradition. My hands are shaking from the adrenaline coursing through my body. I cannot believe I'm getting married today.

At first I was incredibly sad that none of my crew mates or my friends will be here. Then it occurs to me that my relationship with Sam was built mostly through private conversations and game nights on his front room couch. We didn't have huge parties and public events. We fell in love one email, text message and late-night phone conversation at a time. So, I guess it's appropriate that it's only the two of us.

As I slide my foot into the ivory pumps, I encounter a note in the toe. As I pull it out to read it, I chuckle at Jessica's promise of a bodacious party when we are all able to get together. That sounds more like Mitch's friend.

Sam transfers into his scooter and meets me at the bottom of the ramp. "I've never seen you look so beautiful."

"Thank you. You look pretty handsome yourself. I wondered why you were so dressed up just to meet me at the ship. I thought it was because you wanted to look dashing for pictures. I should have known you had an ulterior motive."

Sam grins. "I do want to look dapper for pictures. I just never told you I wanted to look handsome for our wedding pictures."

As we close up the van a gentleman in a black shirt and pants walks up to us with a chair made from PVC pipe with oversized wheels. "Sam Taylor?"

"That's me," Sam answers.

"I thought you might like this. It belongs to my grandson. He uses it when he goes surfing. His regular chair gets stuck in the sand. I thought perhaps you and your fiancé might want to get married on the beach."

Sam looks up at me with wide eyes, "What do you think? I've never really had the option."

"Sounds good to me. It's a beautiful day."

Sam nods at the officiant. "Thank you so much, we would love to get married on the beach."

"I left my notes back at the office. What kind of ceremony were you folks wanting today?"

I look at him steadily in the eye as I answer, "I want it to be as simple as possible. I want to tell Sam I love him, I want to promise him I will love him forever, and I want to hear that he loves me. Beyond that, nothing much matters."

The guy looks at Sam. "Does that sound good to you?"

Sam pulls me toward him so he can kiss me. When he's finished, he answers, "It's perfect."

The officiant tucks in his shirt and smooths back his hair as he motions for us to follow him down toward the beach. "I agree. It sounds like a wonderfully straightforward plan. I love making the dreams of happy couples come true. So, let's turn you into Taylor Taylor, shall we?"

I place my hand on Sam's shoulder as we carefully navigate our way down the winding path to the beach.

That's how I found my port in the storm by knocking down a perfect stranger while I was taking a picture.

Life is funny that way.

THE END

The Hidden Hearts Series continues with Love is More Than Skin Deep.

NOTE FROM THE AUTHOR

Dear Reader,

Thanks for giving this little novella a read. If you liked reading about people who are not so stereotypical, then I've got good news…

…there's more.

The Hidden Hearts Series continues with Love is More Than Skin Deep.

Life is never simple.

Shelby Lyons wanted to get a tattoo to celebrate her accomplishment of becoming a teacher.

Little did she know her impulsive move would change the course of her life.

Mark Littleson has his hands full owning a law firm and raising a daughter with autism on his own. He doesn't need any complications.

Yet, when he witnesses Shelby's breakdown in the middle of Ink'd Deep, he feels compelled to help.

Far from being a complication, Shelby is the piece of the puzzle he and his daughter have been missing.

When Shelby's health is in question, will Mark learn that love is more than skin deep?

(This story is inspired by the heroic journey against skin cancer fought by Judy Noble Cloud.)

Get Love is More Than Skin Deep in paperback, e-book version or read it through Kindle Unlimited now.

~Mary

Because love matters, differences don't.

ACKNOWLEDGEMENTS

No one ever writes in a vacuum. In this project, I had wonderful outside experts. I'd like to thank Scott, Richard, Lacie, Kathern, Heather, Ada and specifically, my husband, Leonard, for his wonderful story idea.

Portions of this version of Port in the Storm were released in the Passion in Portland anthology earlier in 2016. The anthology was conceived to benefit Bradley Angle which is a program in Portland Oregon which helps victims of domestic violence.

Thank you AJ Harmon and Heather Carver for the opportunity to participate in the Passion in Portland anthology. I have spent many years as civil rights advocate and I view my writing as one more extension of that work. It was a wonderful experience.

RESOURCES

If you need help immediately, call 911.

National Sexual Assault Hotline:
1-800-656-HOPE (4673)

National Domestic Violence Hotline:
800-799-SAFE (7233) or 800-787-3224 (TDD)

Domestic Shelters.org— A tool that enables you to find a domestic violence shelter in your area by ZIP Code or address. You can search by the specific service you need. There are also informative articles about how to help someone who may be a victim of domestic violence or sexual abuse.

RAINN (Rape, Abuse, Incest National Network) — The nation's largest anti-sexual assault organization. RAINN operates the National Sexual Assault Hotline at 1.800.656.HOPE and the National Sexual Assault Online Hotline at rainn.org, and publicizes the hotline's free, confidential services; educates the public about sexual assault; and leads national efforts to prevent sexual assault, improve services to victims and ensure that rapists are brought to justice.

Take Back The Night—Media links, literature and other

information about surviving and preventing date rape. Many of these resources are beneficial for helping survivors as well as their family and friends through the healing process.

When Georgia Smiled—A Foundation created by Robin McGraw to create and advance programs that help victims of domestic violence and sexual assault live healthy, safe and joy-filled lives. Initiatives include a phone app that helps create a safety plan for use in domestic violence date rape situations, education initiatives for use in high school and college settings and support programs for women.

Loveisrespect.org— Our mission is to engage, educate and empower young people to prevent and end abusive relationships. Highly-trained peer advocates offer support, information and advocacy to young people who have questions or concerns about their dating relationships. We also provide information and support to concerned friends and family members, teachers, counselors, service providers and members of law enforcement. Free and confidential phone, live chat and texting services are available 24/7/365.

Bradley Angle—The domestic violence program in Portland Oregon for which this anthology is raising funds. It provides comprehensive emergency assistance and ongoing education including programs designed to help members of the LBGT community who have been victims of violence.

ABOUT THE AUTHOR

I have been lucky enough to live my own version of a romance novel. I married the guy who kissed me at summer camp. He told me on the night we met that he was going to marry me and be the father of my children.

Eventually, I stopped giggling when he said it, and we've been married for more than thirty years. We have two children. The oldest is a Doctor of Osteopathy. He is across the United States completing his residency, but when he's done, he is going to come back to Oregon and practice Family Medicine. Our youngest son is now tackling high school and where he is an honor student. He is interested in becoming an EMT.

I write full time now. I have published more than thirty books and have several more underway. I volunteer my time to a variety of causes. I have worked as a Civil Rights Attorney and diversity advocate. I spent several years working for various social service agencies before becoming an attorney.

In my spare time, I love to cook, decorate cakes and of course, I obsessively, compulsively read.

I would be honored if you would take a few moments out of your busy day to check out my website,

MaryCrawfordAuthor.com. While you're there, you can sign up for my newsletter and get a free book. I will be announcing my upcoming books and giving sneak peeks as well as sponsoring giveaways and giving you information about other interesting events.

If you have questions or comments, please E-mail me at Mary@MaryCrawfordAuthor.com or find me on the following social networks:

Facebook: www.facebook.com/authormarycrawford

Website: MaryCrawfordAuthor.com

Twitter: www.twitter.com/MaryCrawfordAut

www.ingramcontent.com/pod-product-compliance
Lightning Source LLC
Chambersburg PA
CBHW032051180726
48284CB00004B/1286